Licensed exclusively to Top That Publishing Ltd
Tide Mill Way, Woodbridge, Suffolk, IP12 1AP, UK
www.topthatpublishing.com
Copyright © 2015 Tide Mill Media
All rights reserved
0 2 4 6 8 9 7 5 3 1
Manufactured in China

Written by Ellie Wharton
Illustrated by Dubravka Kolanovic

ISBN 978-1-78445-249-0

A catalogue record for this book is available from the British Library

Little Lost Panda

By

Ellie Wharton

Little Panda loved running ahead
of Mummy Panda in the
bamboo forest.

'Come back!'

Mummy Panda was always shouting.

One day, Little Panda ran further
than he had ever done before.
He ran so far that he lost the path,
and although he waited and
waited for Mummy Panda's call,
it never came.

Little Panda was lost!

Little Panda sat down in a clearing
and rubbed his eyes with his furry paws.
He wanted Mummy Panda to be there
when he opened them. Instead,
a little bird was sitting on his shoulder.

'What's the matter, Little Panda?'
asked the little bird.

'I've lost my mummy and I'm all alone!'
sobbed Little Panda.

'Nonsense!' said the little bird.
'You're not alone, I'm here.
And I'm sure I saw something furry
with round ears up ahead.
It might be your mummy …

follow me!'

Little Panda followed the little
bird and before long they heard
a rustle of leaves.

Maybe it was Mummy Panda,
thought Little Panda excitedly.

The rustling stopped abruptly
and a furry head with round ears
poked up through the leaves.

But it wasn't Mummy Panda at all.
It was …

a bamboo rat!

'You're too small to be my mummy!'
said Little Panda disappointedly.

'That's true,' said the bamboo rat,
'but I did see something bigger with
a white face and dark patches around
its eyes in the trees up ahead!'

Little Panda thanked the bamboo rat
and they set off in the direction
he was pointing.

Soon enough, Little Panda spotted something
sitting in a tree with a white face and dark patches
around its eyes. Little Panda climbed up the tree
as fast as he could.

But it wasn't Mummy Panda at all, it was …

a flying red
and white squirrel!

'You're too small and too fast to be my mummy!'
said Little Panda disappointedly.

'I am,' said the flying squirrel,
'but I did see something sitting
quite still by the waterfall up ahead
and it was bigger and furrier too!'

Little Panda thanked the flying squirrel
and they set off in the direction he was pointing.

Very soon Little Panda reached the waterfall, and sure enough, sitting quite still beside it was something big and furry.

But it wasn't Mummy Panda at all, it was …

a golden

snub-nosed monkey!

'You're too golden to be my mummy!'
said Little Panda disappointedly.

'Yes I am,' said the monkey,
'but I did happen to see something black and white and furry
not too far up ahead, at the top of that mountain.'

Little Panda thanked the monkey and they set off
in the direction he was pointing.

Little Panda began to climb the small mountain
and before long he came face to face with
something black and white and furry …

But it wasn't Mummy Panda at all, it was …

a snow leopard!

'Quick, run or he'll eat you!'

shouted the little bird to Little Panda.

Little Panda didn't wait to find out
what the snow leopard had to say.
He turned and he ran and he ran
and he ran until he was completely
out of breath.

Little Panda found himself back in the clearing.

'I'll NEVER find Mummy,' he said miserably
to the little bird. 'I'm all alone!'

'Not ENTIRELY alone,'
said a voice in the trees.

Little Panda looked up and saw two
furry ears poking out from a tree up ahead.
Was it … could it be?

But it wasn't Mummy Panda at all,
it was ...

...a red panda!

'You're NOT Mummy Panda!' said Little Panda,
with tears welling up in his eyes.

'Don't cry,' said the red panda,
coming to sit beside Little Panda.

'Follow me, I know just where she'll be.'

Soon they found the path that Little Panda
had lost and Little Panda heard a familiar voice.

'Come back!' it shouted.

Little Panda ran and he ran and he ran,
straight into the big furry bear hug of Mummy Panda.

'There you are, Little Panda!'
Mummy Panda exclaimed happily.
'You must promise never to run off again.
The forest is a dangerous place for a little lost panda!'

Little Panda nodded. 'I promise!' he said,
thankful to be back in his mummy's arms.

Then Little Panda remembered
the little bird and the red panda
and how kind they had been to him
when he thought he was all alone.

'Mummy Panda?
Can my new friends have a bear hug too?'

'Of course!' said Mummy Panda,
gathering Little Panda and his new friends
into her furry beary arms.

The End